Indian And Divorced...

But It's OK!

9 Ways to Strengthen YOUR Wellbeing

By

Bejal Shah

Acknowledgments

I want to begin by expressing my deepest thanks and gratitude to the most important person in my life—my beautiful son. You continue to be my motivation and strength. It is because of you that I found the courage and determination to carry on and never give up. At one point, you were literally a part of me, and because of you, I am—and will always be—a mother. It is a role and title I am deeply blessed with and immensely proud of.

From one mother to another, I extend my heartfelt gratitude to my own mum for speaking the truth when it mattered most. To my brother—thank you. On the 4th of July 2015, you stood by my side in a pivotal moment, helping me realise that I had options. That insight alone gave me the courage to begin the journey of divorce proceedings.

I am also incredibly grateful to my younger sister for her time, patience, and unwavering support—reading through endless bundles of legal paperwork and emails, and accompanying me to every single hearing. And there were quite a few!

To my angel aunt, now among the angels. Inspired by you, I followed your path into counselling and therapy. You remain always in my thoughts. I wish I had told you how much I loved you. Rest in peace—your pure spirit lives on.

A sincere thank you to my father for providing the financial support I so desperately needed at that time—support I'm proud to say has since been repaid in full. To my older sister and my closest girls (you know who you are)—thank you for never judging me and for always being there in the background, offering your love and strength.

Finally, to my partner—thank you. Together, we've made a fresh start and have already created some beautiful memories. Here's to continuing our journey side by side, building a life filled with love, joy, and unconditional support.

.

To those labelled as 'divorcees':

It is not the label that defines you. Remember who you are; you are so much more than a word or a status. Your story, your strength, and your journey are what truly matter.

Contents

Preface

Dear Reader,

Believe it or not, my initial reason for writing about my experience of going through a messy divorce began as a therapeutic exercise. It was suggested that openly and honestly expressing my feelings could support my healing, so I set out to write about the emotions and experiences I had kept buried inside for so long. The process was meant to be part of my own journey towards recovery.

Now, over seven years on, and with my title restored to "Ms.", I find myself in a very different place—emotionally, physically, mentally, and spiritually. A great deal has happened during that time, and now that I finally have the space to reflect, I have begun to process it all more deeply.

As I started writing down my memories, it quickly became clear that five key goals had emerged from this exercise. For ease, I have listed them here:

1. To use writing as part of my own healing journey
2. To support and offer comfort to anyone in a similar position—or considering divorce—so they know what to expect
3. To raise awareness of the lack of adequate support available during divorce proceedings
4. To highlight the need for a more streamlined and accessible divorce process
5. To use my perspective as a therapist to support others and help build stronger, more inclusive support networks and communities

From my experience, divorcees have always carried a stigma—especially within the culture and community I grew up in. I know that times are changing: divorce rates are rising, and people are becoming more open about their experiences. Yet, the stigma still lingers, and more needs to be done to challenge and shift the narrative.

Through my training as a therapist, I have developed a deep interest in trauma and loss, and I want to explore the connection between divorce and its long-term impact on a person's life, well-being, and relationships. I believe divorce is a form of loss—and for many, like me, it can be a traumatic experience. This is an area that still lacks proper attention and research, but by better understanding what people go through, we can begin to create supportive systems that allow individuals to heal and rebuild with dignity and strength.

While writing, I realised that simply putting my feelings into words helped illuminate parts of my experience that I had never fully understood before. It became a deeply therapeutic process. But I also recognised that my journey could have been made easier if the right support had been available—and that realisation is what sparked the rest of my goals.

So, I truly hope that some good comes from sharing my story—whether it helps someone feel less alone, prepares them for what to expect, or raises awareness about the gaps in support. If even one of those things is achieved, I will feel that my mission has been fulfilled.

Getting the Most Out of This Book

I've written this book with the hope that you can use as much—or as little—as you need to support whatever is most significant to you and your unique situation. Please feel free to jump from chapter to chapter; there is no need to follow a strict order.

Throughout these pages, I've shared a number of strategies that supported my well-being during an especially difficult time in my life. I understand that what worked for me might not work for everyone—we are all wonderfully unique. Take what resonates with you, and gently leave behind what doesn't.

If there is one message I cannot emphasise enough, it is this: **spend time on yourself**. Prioritising yourself is not selfish—it is essential. Only when we take care of our own needs can we meaningfully support others.

My personal mantra has always been: **"health is wealth."** Your well-being is a valuable investment, and the time and energy you dedicate to self-care today will not only benefit you now but also help keep you grounded and resilient in the years ahead.

Each section of this book has been designed with clarity and ease of reading in mind. In places, I've included reflective questions to support your thought processes and encourage deeper self-awareness.

Introduction: Why I Chose to Share My Story

If I'm being totally honest, the main reason I began writing about my experience was because I was completely clueless about divorce and everything it involved. I had no idea what the process looked like or how I was going to cope afterwards. It wasn't something I had ever imagined would happen to me—and the emotional, legal, and practical challenges completely blindsided me.

Writing became my way of making sense of what I was going through. At first, it was just for me: a space to express my experiences and feelings on paper and try to understand them, supporting me towards my own healing. But as I reflected and healed, I realised that I wanted to share my experience in the hope that it might help others who find themselves in a similar position. I wanted to give people a sense of what to expect—emotionally, legally, and financially—and raise awareness about the lack of support that exists within the system. I understand that everyone's journey is unique, and all I can do is share mine honestly and openly.

In the beginning, I really struggled to accept what was happening to me. How could I—me—be getting a divorce? I had always tried to live a good, honest life. I believed that if you did the right thing, good things would come to you. Divorce didn't fit into that narrative. Like so many of us, I grew up believing in the fairytale ending—get married, live happily ever after. Divorce wasn't supposed to be part of the story. Of course, that's a whole other conversation, but it reflects the beliefs many of us are raised with.

At the time, I was overwhelmed—consumed with fears, doubts, and worries. I wasn't just facing the end of a marriage; I was struggling with the shame I felt, the fear of judgement from society, and the worry about what it would mean for my family, my identity, and most importantly, my son. Would I always be labelled a divorcee? Would I be able to live on my own? Would my son be okay? I had what I can only describe as a complete mental overload.

I also think it's important to give some context about my background. I was raised in a culture where divorce is rarely discussed openly. Being of Indian origin, I found that within the Indian community, divorce is often spoken about behind closed doors—or worse, as gossip. There's little support, little understanding, and plenty of judgement. And while attitudes are slowly changing, there is still a long way to go.

This is why I feel so strongly about highlighting the cultural and societal pressures that come with divorce. These pressures can make an already painful situation even harder, especially when you're expected to stay silent or pretend everything is fine.

During the divorce process, I felt like just another number. Yes, I met with a lawyer who explained the costs and steps, but no one ever asked how I was doing emotionally. There was no human connection, no offer of support—just fees, forms, and court dates. What I needed most in that moment was someone. A voice. A guide. Some kind of support network. And it was missing. That absence is something I want to bring real attention to.

Looking back, I can see that one of my main coping strategies was staying busy. At the time, I had a demanding job that kept my mind occupied, and in many ways, that was a blessing. I did not have the space to dwell, so I just kept going. I'm not saying it's the best way, but for me, it helped me survive.

As part of my training to become a therapist, I attended therapy myself, and it was through this process that I began to unpack what had happened and what had helped me get through it. With time and guidance, I understood my own experience more deeply, and it's this understanding that I now want to share with others.

So, the true purpose of writing this memoir is simple:

- To offer support and comfort to others navigating divorce
- To share what I've learned and what to expect
- To raise awareness about the gaps in support systems—legal, emotional, and cultural
- And to help break the silence that too often surrounds divorce in our communities

Even if this helps just one person feel less alone, or gives them the courage to ask for help, then I will consider it a success. Because for me, even a small impact would be huge.

Part I – The System(s)

Chapter One: Divorce Proceedings and What to Expect

I'm going to dive straight into the divorce proceedings themselves—what to expect, how the process unfolds, and what sort of timescales and practical considerations may be involved. My hope is that by sharing my experience, I can offer you some clarity, support, and reassurance.

When I began my divorce journey, I had no idea what to expect. I didn't know the cost, the steps, the timelines—nothing. I was completely overwhelmed, emotionally drained, and, if I'm honest, in a state of shock. It's possible these things were explained to me at the time, but I simply do not remember. What I do remember is feeling incredibly alone. My future—one I had envisioned as a married woman, a wife, part of a unit—had suddenly crumbled, and everything around me was changing.

In hindsight (and hindsight really is a wonderful thing), I realise that I went into autopilot mode. I continued going to work. I took care of my young child. I did the cooking, cleaning, laundry—everything I was used to doing. I just kept going. I had to. But emotionally, I had completely suppressed what I was feeling just to make it through the day.

And that is one of the biggest reasons I am writing this now. If you're in a similar situation, or even just considering divorce, I want you to know that you're not alone. You do not have to figure this out in silence. By explaining what I went through, I hope I can give you a sense of the process and what to expect. More importantly, I want to raise awareness of how little emotional and mental support is available during this time—and how vital it is.

From a legal perspective, I was told what to do—what paperwork to complete, what forms to sign, what the next steps were. But no one ever asked how I was doing. There was no offer of emotional support from my solicitor, nor from the family court. And yet, this was a profound loss—a loss of identity, of status, of hopes and dreams I once held. For me, it was traumatic.

One of my hopes in sharing this is that one day, meaningful support will be embedded into the divorce process—not just legal guidance, but emotional care as well. Ideally, the system itself will become more compassionate and easier to navigate. For me, the process was complex, slow, and draining—and anything that can make it easier for those going through it would be a positive step.

Because I had a young child—under the age of five at the time—my divorce involved three distinct legal stages. These were separate processes but closely linked. If I hadn't had a child, the process would have looked very different, and I wouldn't have needed to go through Child Arrangements at all.

The three stages I experienced were:

1. **Child Arrangements**
2. **Financial Arrangements**
3. **The Divorce itself** (often referred to as the Decree Absolute)

Each of these came with its own challenges, paperwork, court dates, and emotional strain. In the following sections, I'll explain each one from my personal perspective—what happened, how it felt, and what I wish I had known at the time.

My Top Tips

- Are you currently considering divorce? What are the reasons behind this? Try to identify and name them clearly.
- Do you have someone close—a trusted friend or family member—with whom you can speak honestly about your feelings?
- Can you have an open, honest conversation with your spouse about your concerns? Would you both consider professional support, such as couples counselling?

Is it time to start researching legal representation, even just to understand your rights and options?

Chapter Two: Child Arrangements and What to Expect

When children are involved in a divorce—particularly those under 18—the first legal consideration is usually Child Arrangements. This was certainly true in my case, as my son was under the age of five when I began divorce proceedings.

What Are Child Arrangements?

Child Arrangements determine:

- Who the child will live with
- How time is shared between parents
- Who holds responsibility for important decisions concerning the child's welfare

When parents cannot reach an agreement themselves, the matter is escalated to the Family Court, where a judge makes a legally binding Child Arrangement Order.

If a child is old enough to express their views, these may be taken into account. However, my son was too young, so all decisions were made by the court based on legal arguments and what was believed to be in his best interests.

Beginning the Process

When I confirmed with my solicitor that I wanted a divorce, she submitted the initial request to the Family Court to begin the Child

Arrangements process. I had no prior knowledge of how any of this worked, so I relied heavily on her guidance.

The legal process usually involves up to three hearings, with the hope that parents can come to an agreement during one of them. If an agreement is reached at any stage, the court formalises it into a court order. If not, the judge makes the final decision at the third and final hearing.

My First Hearing

I was anxious—terrified, even—on the day of the first hearing. I remember changing outfits several times before settling on something that felt "okay enough." I had no idea what to expect. Thankfully, my cousin sister came with me for support. Walking into the Family Court in London, going through security, having my bags checked, and being told to find a free room all felt overwhelming.

We eventually found a small, dimly lit room with a table and a few chairs. The atmosphere was cold and clinical. When my solicitor arrived, she explained the process: she would attempt to negotiate with my husband's legal representative before we were called into court.

No agreement was reached. When we were finally called, we simply reported that no resolution had been found. The judge scheduled a second hearing. I left feeling like just another number—processed and passed along.

Second Hearing: Familiarity Doesn't Ease the Pain

The second hearing followed the same pattern. The building and the process were now familiar, but that didn't make anything easier. Despite my cousin's continued support, the experience remained cold and isolating.

Again, no agreement was reached, and a third final hearing was scheduled.

Third and Final Hearing

The final hearing was emotionally and physically exhausting. We spent the entire day trying to reach an agreement. Everyone—myself included—was drained.

Eventually, we reached a settlement, which the court approved. But even as I agreed to it, a part of me was breaking. The idea of not being with my son every day, after having been with him since birth, was devastating. I tried to remain composed, but inside, I felt powerless.

I believe in fairness and shared parenting, but having been the primary carer, I struggled with the outcome. I often wonder whether I should have been more emotional or assertive, but at that point, I was simply exhausted.

A Call for Better Support

One of the most glaring issues throughout this process was the complete lack of emotional or mental health support. No one asked how I was coping. No one offered guidance or resources to help me manage the overwhelming emotions. I was lucky to have my cousin—but many people go through this alone.

Timeline and Reflections

My Child Arrangements process began in January 2016 and concluded in August 2016—eight months that felt like a lifetime. While some might say eight months isn't long, when you're living through uncertainty and heartbreak, it absolutely is.

Once Child Arrangements were finalised, I was finally able to move out of the marital home and live with my parents while the remaining divorce proceedings continued. Living under the same roof during those eight months added an extra layer of stress—something that should be acknowledged in conversations about emotional wellbeing during divorce.

Final Thoughts

If you don't have children, or your children are adults, this part of the process won't apply to you. But for those who do, I hope sharing my experience helps paint a clearer picture of what to expect—and highlights how essential proper emotional support is during divorce.

No one should have to feel as isolated and emotionally neglected as I did. With greater awareness and better systems in place, I hope we can change that—for ourselves and for those who come after us.

My Top Tips

- Reflect on how the separation may affect your child(ren) emotionally and practically.

- Consider seeking professional guidance or trusted resources on how to approach conversations with your children in an age-appropriate manner.
- Write down your initial thoughts about what you believe childcare arrangements should look like—and why.

Preparing in advance can help you approach the process more calmly and thoughtfully, centred on your child(ren)'s best interests.

Chapter Three: Financial Arrangements and What to Expect

The next stage I went through was the Financial Arrangement process, which was quite similar to the Child Arrangements process. In both cases, the aim is for both parties to reach an agreement—ideally with the help of legal representatives who negotiate on your behalf. Once an agreement is reached, it is submitted to the Family Court for approval. If no agreement is possible, the court ultimately makes the decision.

My financial situation at the time was not strong. I had previously owned a business, but I sold it just before my son was born because I couldn't manage both the demands of running a business and caring for a newborn. The sale didn't result in any profit, leaving me with very little savings.

Looking back, I realise I was not very financially aware. My husband handled all financial matters—his area of expertise—while I focused on the home and childcare. I now feel disappointed in myself for not being more involved, especially since I had previously bought, sold, and managed property independently. Perhaps it was a lack of confidence, or simply the fact that financial literacy wasn't discussed or taught when I was younger. In hindsight, I wish I had taken more interest in it.

If there is one piece of advice I would offer anyone, it's this: take an active interest in your finances, no matter who is "better" at it. And if you don't feel confident, take the time to learn. Financial literacy is empowering and essential—especially during major life transitions like divorce.

During this stage, I relied heavily on my legal representative. One thing I learned is that living arrangements are assessed based on need—not on what you previously had. For example, even though our marital home had four bedrooms, the court decided that a two- or three-bedroom home would be suitable for me.

Because my income was low, the court granted me a financial allowance to be paid by my ex-husband for a set number of years. However, this payment stopped quickly. What I didn't know at the time was that I would have needed to return to court to reinstate it. I simply didn't have the emotional energy to do so, but I share this now so that others know to ask the right questions and understand their rights.

The financial arrangements were resolved relatively quickly, with delays mainly due to waiting for responses from legal representatives. Once an agreement was made, it was approved by the court and became legally binding. The settlement is finalised after the Decree Absolute is granted, and your legal team handles this stage.

My Top Tips

- Review your personal finances carefully—list all income and expenses to understand your current situation clearly.
- Consider seeking professional financial advice to understand your options more fully.
- Factor in any potential legal costs if you're working with a solicitor or mediator.

- Outline what you would need financially to live independently, including childcare, housing, and daily living costs.

Reflect on advice from legal and financial professionals to help you make informed decisions.

Chapter Four: The Divorce Itself – aka Decree Absolute

The final stage of the legal process is obtaining the Decree Absolute, which officially ends the marriage. In theory, this stage is straightforward: you file your application for divorce with the court, and if there are no objections, the court processes it and issues the Decree Absolute, confirming that you are no longer legally married.

In my case, the Decree Absolute came at the end of the entire process. First, we dealt with Child Arrangements, then Financial Arrangements, and only once these were resolved could I apply.

When the court grants your Decree Absolute, they send an official letter. It's important to keep all your legal documents safe. For example, I needed mine to change my passport back to my maiden name. I also carry a copy when travelling with my son, as our surnames differ, in case I need to prove that I am his mother.

Timeframe

To give you a sense of the timeline: I began legal proceedings in January 2016 and was legally divorced in December 2017. I received the paperwork in January 2018. From start to finish, the process took almost two years. It was long, emotionally draining, and filled with court hearings, meetings with legal representatives, and countless hours reviewing documents.

Of course, every case is different. If there are no children involved, and if both parties agree quickly on finances and childcare, the process can be faster. I know families who did not use solicitors for everything—they agreed on finances and childcare privately and only sought legal support to formalise the divorce, reducing time and cost significantly.

In my case, most of my costs came from legal fees due to the complexity and length of the proceedings.

My Top Tips

- Prioritise self-care. You've been through something significant—allow yourself rest and reflection.
- Be compassionate with yourself. It's natural to feel a wide range of emotions. Healing is not linear.

You may choose to update personal documents (such as name changes or titles). There's no rush—do this when you feel ready.

Chapter Five: The Financial Cost Involved in a Divorce

I felt this topic deserved its own section—because, let's be honest, everything has a price, and divorce is no exception. I want to share my experience to help others understand not only the timelines but also the realistic financial cost involved.

Every interaction I had with my legal representative came with a fee. Emails, calls, meetings, document reviews—everything was billed. Over two years, these fees added up significantly. And that does not include travel costs, printing, or other smaller expenses that accumulate quietly over time.

One thing that surprised me was the lack of information about financial or legal aid. I'm not sure if this was because I sourced my solicitor privately, but I don't recall being told about any assistance. I simply assumed I had to pay for everything myself.

At the time, I worked in education—a rewarding field, but not one known for high pay. I had a steady income, but it was limited. Solicitors expect invoices to be paid promptly, and failure to do so can result in your representation being paused or withdrawn. I ended up borrowing money to continue. Thankfully, I was able to repay that loan, which I did with pride. Rebuilding my financial life became a priority.

For many people, the cost alone can influence whether they pursue a divorce. If you need legal support—as I did—be prepared: divorce is expensive. When I made the decision to leave my marriage, money wasn't even on my mind. I had emotionally left the relationship.

Everything else—money, logistics, stress—I decided to deal with as it came. In hindsight, this approach had its pros and cons.

My hope in sharing this is to increase awareness of the need for better financial guidance and support structures. There should be bursaries, legal aid, or at minimum, clearer advice available—especially for those who cannot afford to leave an unhappy or unsafe situation.

Divorce is emotionally and mentally exhausting. The financial burden only adds to the stress. I wish I had received more support—and I hope that by sharing my story, someone else might feel better prepared.

My Top Tips

- Review your finances carefully. Knowing your income and expenses gives clarity and control.
- If needed, consider temporary support such as a loan from someone you trust—with clear repayment terms.
- Build financial confidence. Explore courses, online resources, or local support to improve financial literacy and independence.

Chapter Six: Mediation

I wanted to include a section on mediation, as I recall it being part of the process, almost like ticking a box, before officially requesting a divorce. It is often required or strongly encouraged by the court to see whether any part of the separation (childcare, finances, or communication) can be resolved outside of court with the help of a neutral third party.

In theory, mediation can be a very helpful space. It gives both parties the chance to talk openly and honestly with an independent mediator who is there to facilitate discussion and support mutual agreements. For many couples, it can be a more cost-effective and less confrontational route.

However, I want to be honest about my own experience, which, unfortunately, was very negative. The mediator I saw came across as cold and unapproachable. There was no sense of warmth or empathy, no human connection that made me feel heard or supported. As a result, I felt completely unable to open up or engage in a meaningful way. The whole session left me drained and upset, and I walked away feeling that it had been a waste of time, money, and emotional energy.

I fully acknowledge that there are likely many excellent, compassionate mediators who do a fantastic job in supporting separating couples. I have heard of people having positive and even transformative experiences through meditation. Sadly, that was not the case for me.

So, my advice would be this: do your research if you are going down the mediation route. Do not be afraid to ask questions beforehand, or even request a different mediator if you feel the one you are working with is not a good fit. Like any professional relationship, rapport and trust matter, especially when emotions are high and the stakes are personal.

My Top Tips

- Your legal representative may be able to recommend trusted mediators, but it is also a good idea to do your own research to find someone you feel comfortable with.
- If your first mediation session does not feel productive, or you are not satisfied with the approach, you have every right to try a different mediator. Finding the right fit can make a big difference.
- Remember, mediation is a space for both parties to attempt to reach mutual agreements. However, it does not mean you must agree. Sometimes, despite best efforts, agreement is not possible, and that is okay. This is why the legal system includes formal court processes as a next step when mediation is not successful.

Chapter Seven: Support and How Important Support Is

I have spoken earlier about the importance of having support, but I want to expand on this, because for me, this is one of the most crucial parts of navigating a divorce. One of my key reasons for writing this book is to raise awareness about how vital it is to have support when going through, or even just considering, a divorce.

Support is part of self-care, and I feel so strongly about this that I have dedicated an entire chapter to ways support can be implemented and accessed.

My Experience with Lack of Support

Throughout my own divorce, I was not offered any emotional or well-being support. No one checked in with me to ask how I was coping, not my solicitor and not the Family Court. I went through the entire process feeling completely alone.

By sharing my experience, I hope no one else has to feel that isolated. At a minimum, I believe some consideration for well-being support should be available to anyone going through a legal separation. If I could influence change and make such support mandatory at all stages of the process, then sharing my story would have been worth it.

What Support Could Look Like

Support can take many forms. Here are some suggestions that I believe could have made a real difference during my own experience:

- Access to counselling or therapy

- One-on-one support to help explain the divorce process and what to expect
- Financial planning guidance
- Emotional support or information for the wider family, especially children
- Signposting to community networks or support groups where shared experiences can help

I understand that implementing such resources may depend on funding and availability. But even if solicitors or the courts cannot offer these services directly, they could at least signpost individuals to external resources.

The Role of Employers

Another valuable source of support can come from your workplace. If you are employed, I highly recommend speaking with your Human Resources (HR) department or manager to find out what support is available.

In my case, I worked in HR and had a strong relationship with my line manager. This helped me access flexibility around childcare and appointments, as well as emotional support through work's Employee Assistance Programme (EAP).

EAPs are confidential services often included in company insurance plans. They typically offer:

- Free counselling sessions (many offer six sessions)
- Access to helplines for legal or financial advice
- Informational resources on mental health and well-being
- Call-back services for professional support at a convenient time

Using my employer's EAP gave me clarity and reassurance. It was especially helpful when solicitor meetings became overwhelming. I could speak with someone who explained things in clear, simple terms, without the pressure of time or legal fees. That space helped me understand the process better and feel a little less alone.

Therapy: Then and Now

Seven years on, I now deeply value the importance of therapy, especially after experiencing it myself as part of my training to become a therapist. Talking to someone in a safe, non-judgemental space can make a world of difference, particularly when you are carrying heavy emotional weight with no one to confide in.

Looking back, I wish I had reached out sooner. I stayed in *autopilot mode*, functioning on the outside while struggling internally. Therapy has helped me process that experience, understand my grief, and begin healing. I now see my divorce for what it was: a traumatic loss, and like any loss, it deserved to be grieved properly.

If your workplace does not offer EAP services, you can seek private counselling through resources such as the BACP Counselling Directory, which allows you to search for therapists who meet your specific needs. While private therapy comes with a cost, I truly believe it is a worthwhile investment in your mental and emotional health.

GP and Community Support

Do not forget that your GP (General Practitioner) can also be a valuable point of contact. They may be able to offer referrals, provide mental health support, or point you towards additional resources available in your area.

Family and Friends: Your Inner Circle

If you have trusted family members or friends, your inner circle, consider opening up to them. Speaking your truth, even just a little, can ease the emotional load.

At the time, I did not feel I could talk to my family. I take ownership of that. It was partly due to our family dynamics, but I also believe cultural factors played a role, which I will explore in the next chapter. I felt misunderstood, and I was the first in my family to go through a divorce, so I had no one to compare my experience to or confide in.

I also did not fully open up to my closest friends. I did not want to burden anyone. Everyone had their own problems and their own lives. So I kept it all to myself, and my thoughts just circled endlessly in my mind. Outwardly, I appeared strong and composed. Inwardly, I was barely holding it together.

In Reflection

I now realise that writing this book has been part of my own healing process. Personal therapy, which I undertook as part of my training, allowed me to unpack and understand my experience on a much deeper level. My therapist was warm, attuned, and truly present with me, and it is my hope that I can offer the same presence to my future clients.

Final Thoughts

Support matters. Whether it comes from a professional, a friend, an employer, or even just a helpful resource, having someone in your corner can make a world of difference when you are going through something as life-altering as a divorce.

If my words encourage even one person to seek support, or if they prompt changes in how legal systems or workplaces approach support, then I will feel this chapter, and this book, have done something meaningful.

In the next chapter, I will explore how culture and expectations can shape the way we experience and cope with divorce, especially when it comes to silence, stigma, and the pressure to "hold it together".

My Top Tips

- Self-care is not selfish. It is essential for your well-being. Taking time to care for yourself allows you to show up more fully in other areas of your life.
- Seeking support is a strength, not a weakness. Reaching out shows self-awareness and courage. No one is meant to go through everything alone.
- Therapy can be a powerful tool. If you do not feel a connection with a therapist, that is okay. Keep looking until you find the right fit. (Speaking from personal experience, it made a real difference for me.)
- Reflect on what support truly means to you. Consider what helps you feel grounded, safe, and well. This might include people, practices, boundaries, or routines. Your definition of support is valid.

Chapter Eight: My Growing Up and Background

I am British-born, have lived in Britain all my life, and continue to reside here to this day. My parents, on the other hand, migrated from Kenya, Africa, in the 1960s. They got married and settled in the UK. I am one of four children. Sadly, my first brother passed away at the age of two when I was just three. Although I do not remember him, the loss of any family member impacts everyone in the family, consciously and unconsciously.

Growing up, like many Indians of my generation, the message was clear: get a good job and be educated. This meant study, study, and more study. Education was key. You had to work hard to get good grades, which would allow you to attend a reputable university. Depending on your career path, you could then study further for a Master's, PhD, or other higher qualifications. A good education would lead to a good job, which would lead to good pay, and that would mean a comfortable life without financial struggle.

I remember when I was young, being a doctor was considered a highly respected career. I also recall the pressure to get only As in school, as that was seen as proof you were clever. Now, looking back, times have certainly changed. The grading system has shifted from letters to numbers, and there is greater recognition that academic success alone does not determine a person's knowledge or success in life.

I understand why education was so important to my parents. Their upbringing was tough. Both their parents, my grandparents, were unable to complete their education because they had to earn money and work to put food on the table. My parents were fortunate to be offered the opportunity to travel abroad to find a better life, but this meant leaving their birth country. So, it is no surprise they believed education was the key to success. Naturally, this became my belief as well when I was younger.

Reflecting on my journey, I believe times have changed for the better regarding education. There are now many more options available, including various professional qualifications and routes to success. Careers have diversified hugely. You can even become a professional influencer now, something unheard of when I was growing up.

Once education is behind you, the next stage, according to family and cultural expectations, is to settle down, get married, and have children. From a parent's point of view, this means their child is settled, and the family cycle continues. So, you teach your children the same way you were taught. At the time, it certainly felt that if you did not follow this path, something was wrong with you. Looking back, I realise I followed exactly that path.

I studied, got my degree, and even completed a Master's qualification. I started my career and worked my way up. I was so focused on my career that I was not actively looking for a partner. But by the time I was nearing 30, considered "old" in the Indian community, I started looking and eventually met my now ex-husband online. After dating a few times, we told our families and got married within a year. He had been married before, but that marriage was annulled. I was open-minded about this, but looking back, perhaps I should have considered his previous marriage more carefully, or even lived together before marrying. However, living together before marriage would not have been allowed by my parents.

To add to this, among my friends, I was the only one unmarried at that age, so I also felt pressure within myself. A year into the marriage, and through IVF, I had my son. At that time, having a baby was very important because I was aware of my biological clock. Even though there were things in my marriage that made me uncomfortable, my focus shifted to preparing to be a mum.

After my son's birth, it became clearer that I was increasingly unhappy in my marriage. I was not just married to my husband. I felt married to his parents and sister as well, which made things even harder.

When I finally decided to pursue a divorce, it was not common within my family or social circle. I did not know anyone close who had gone through a divorce. The first thing I wondered was: What will my parents think? Would I be ostracised by my family, community, or society? What about my son? How would he be treated?

I had many internal conversations trying to understand why this was happening. I had done everything "right" according to the path I described, so how could this happen to me?

When my son was about two, I told my parents I was struggling. This was incredibly hard because I felt embarrassed, ashamed, and guilty. I suppose it was a shock to them, too. I was the first to get married in our family, so this was new territory.

I kept trying to make the marriage work for the sake of my son and family, despite my doubts. But eventually, I reached my breaking point. I realised I did not want to stay in a marriage where I was not valued or respected. Loyalty, trust, and honesty are core to me. These were missing.

I summoned the courage, even though at the time I did not feel brave, and told myself I would face whatever consequences came my way. I had to be true to myself, even though I was terrified.

I was clear about my decision and what I wanted from the end of the marriage. I remember telling my brother, "This is it. I want out," and the relief was immense.

Outwardly, I kept functioning day to day, but inside, I was in turmoil, emotional, angry, scared, alone, and vulnerable.

After deciding to divorce, I put everything else on hold to focus on the process. I knew it would affect my son, my family, and break cultural and societal traditions. But by then, I realised my own well-being and self-respect were most important. Only then could I truly support my son and others.

Starting the process, I worried less about what others thought. Yes, I would be gossip for a day, then something else would replace me. I had the support of my brother and mum. Just hearing them say they stood with me gave me the courage to take that first step.

But the reality was that I had to do it alone. I had to confront the situation, find a solicitor, and begin proceedings, all while living in the same house and trying to act normal for my son. It was incredibly difficult. The home became hostile.

Schedules for my son's care were imposed and later presented in court as the norm, which shocked me.

This period was far from what I expected growing up. I wanted to minimise risk and protect my child. Having studied psychology, I knew early childhood was crucial to development. I wanted my son to feel secure with me, so I accepted the care schedules calmly, not fighting or arguing. This was not weakness or cowardice. I was choosing tolerance to protect my child's well-being and maintain peace at home.

Complicating matters further, my brother announced his wedding plans around the same time. I decided to wait until after his wedding, in July 2015, to start formal divorce proceedings, which I began in January 2016.

Indian weddings are big celebrations, especially since my brother was the only boy, and this would be the family's last wedding. The planning kept me busy and, in some ways, supported me emotionally. I do not regret waiting, though it was a very challenging period.

Soon after Child Arrangements were decided, I had to move back in with my parents due to financial constraints. This brought new challenges. I was still going through divorce proceedings while caring for my son and trying to keep things normal and fun, all while knowing he would soon leave to stay with his dad.

When my parents had friends over, I felt shame and guilt. It seemed like everyone was silently judging, unwilling to acknowledge the "elephant in the room". At that time, divorce was still considered taboo.

Divorce is more accepted now, but I carried guilt and shame for a long time. Only through personal therapy and time to process my experience have I come to accept that I needed to grieve. My divorce was traumatic, and I will discuss grief and loss more in the next chapter.

Reflecting on my upbringing and culture, I realise I was breaking traditions by divorcing, the first in my family and social circle. This brought much guilt and shame. But being born and educated in the West has its advantages. It helps you see what is acceptable and what is not.

Today, I do not regret my decision. While I am more spiritual than religious now, I respect my faith and understand that culture, religion, and society are complex, integrated communities with evolving expectations and traditions.

My Top Tips

- Reflect on your upbringing. Consider how your early experiences have shaped your current views, beliefs, and behaviours. Awareness of this can help you understand yourself more deeply.
- Explore your values and beliefs. What do you truly believe in today? Have these evolved over time, or stayed the same? Growth often involves re-examining our core principles.
- Acknowledge different perspectives. We all see the world through different lenses. Accepting this diversity of viewpoints can foster empathy and reduce conflict.
- Recognise that change is difficult. Change, even when positive, can feel uncomfortable. Give yourself space to adjust at your own pace.

- Practise self-compassion and kindness. You are a work in progress, just like everyone else. Treat yourself with the same care and patience you would offer a friend.

PART II: Change, Well-being and Meaning/Purpose

In this next section, I want to turn the focus inward, to really explore my own well-being and what has given my life meaning. Writing about my experiences so far has reminded me just how far I have come, and how much inner strength we all carry within ourselves.

Reflecting on what helped me navigate such a difficult and traumatic time, certain things stood out as vital sources of support and meaning. These reflections felt deeply relevant to me, and so I want to share them with you, in the hope that they might offer some comfort, inspiration, or guidance on your own journey.

Chapter Nine: Grief, Loss, and Trauma

I believe it is so important to include grief and loss here because recognising and being able to grieve your losses is crucial to moving forward in life. Without acceptance of loss, healing is difficult.

Through my training in therapy, I have come to understand that my divorce was indeed a form of loss. I lost my status as a married woman and reverted to being single. I also lost my marital home, a home I had built and worked hard to create for my family. Perhaps most deeply, I lost the sense of belonging to that family unit.

The Oxford Learner's Dictionaries defines loss as "the state of no longer having something or as much of something, the process that leads to this, or the death of a person". For me, this broad definition helps me now accept my divorce as a loss. I used to believe loss only referred to losing a loved one, but I now understand it can take many forms: loss of a job, loss of health, loss of a home, and so forth.

My interest in grief and loss led me to volunteer with Cruse Bereavement Support during my placement to become an accredited therapist. The training and induction I received were delivered with compassion and professionalism. Having experienced deep personal loss, I find I can hold space for my clients and support them through their own periods of loss.

I have mentioned before how hindsight is a wonderful thing. At the time of my divorce, I was operating on autopilot, simply getting through each day. I did not have time to process my feelings or talk to anyone. I had a demanding full-time job and was a single parent doing everything alone, all while navigating divorce proceedings.

It is only now, in a better mental and emotional space, that I have had the time and capacity to process what happened to me. My decision to train as a therapist has been invaluable in this journey. Through personal therapy, I have unpacked much of my experience and gained a deeper understanding of myself. I learned the significance of grieving one's loss because, if left unprocessed, grief festers within.

I am not sure why I did not see my divorce as a loss at the time. Perhaps this is cultural, but I do not know for sure. My training and placement, however, have given me a much greater understanding of grief, loss, and trauma.

My journey has taught me that grieving has no set timeline. Grief remains with you, but you must be willing to acknowledge your loss and allow yourself to mourn without shame or guilt. This acceptance is essential to healing.

It has taken me over seven years to fully accept my divorce as a loss. This process was partly helped by my studies and personal therapy. Now that I have spoken about it openly, I feel free in a way I never did before. I no longer feel trapped by it.

This is why I wanted to include this section here. I strongly believe it is vital to grieve and accept your losses. Without this, you hold on to pain inside, and you cannot truly move forward freely in life.

Everyone grieves differently. Some prefer to grieve privately, others find comfort in trusted friends or family, and some choose to explore their grief in therapy. Whatever your way, choose what feels best for you.

My Top Tips

- Take time to reflect on your loss. Have you given yourself space to grieve? Sometimes, in trying to stay strong, we overlook the need to truly process what we have lost.
- Consider seeking professional support. Talking to someone experienced in bereavement, loss, or trauma can help you better understand your emotions and find a path through them.
- Grief has no set timeline. Everyone grieves in their own way and at their own pace. There is no "right" way to grieve, and it is okay to feel differently from others.

Chapter Ten: Self-Respect and Self-Worth

The first thing that comes to mind when reflecting on my journey is the importance of self-respect, recognising that I am important in my own right. If I could not learn to love and respect myself, how could I expect others to do the same? Somewhere along the course of my marriage and divorce, I lost sight of myself and my own self-worth. Looking back, I attribute this to the emotional overload I was carrying and the negative thoughts on repeat, blaming myself, all of which fuelled feelings of low self-worth and dislike for who I had become.

Being in a family or relationship where you are dismissed or not respected deeply impacts your confidence and how you value yourself. During my therapist training, I learned about Bowlby's theory of the secure base, and it resonated with me. Growing up surrounded by encouragement, love, and support helps build a secure and confident individual, or at least a network to lean on when things are not right. But during my divorce, I was far from confident. Outwardly, I might have appeared okay, but inside, I knew I was not.

At that time, I also started to explore my faith more deeply, perhaps as a way to keep busy, but also out of genuine curiosity. I discovered that self-respect is a gem within my faith, a crucial foundation to valuing and respecting others.

Anyone who has experienced divorce knows it is painful and stressful. For me, anxiety and stress were constant companions, and I might have been depressed too, though I never sought medical help. I remember hiding from the world and neglecting my appearance. My cousin took me shopping to boost my confidence, and yes, dressing well helped me feel better, especially during court appearances, but true confidence comes from within, and I had a long way to go.

I wrestled with low self-worth daily, questioning my abilities endlessly. Situations like court hearings and meetings with lawyers were overwhelming, making me want to cry, but I held it together to appear strong. Often, I was on autopilot, just surviving each day. Looking back, I wish I had therapy then, an outlet to process those feelings instead of bottling them up.

My faith kept me grounded, helping me accept and respect myself more. This was my first turning point in personal growth. I wish I had had someone to talk to, to help me work through those thoughts and emotions.

Change did not happen overnight. It is easy to let others' words and actions chip away at your self-worth. After all, no one likes negative feedback. We all crave praise to support our ego. Even now, I am my own biggest critic. But therapy and faith have taught me that thoughts and words are just that. They are not facts.

Believing in myself was difficult during that time, but I reminded myself of all I had achieved, linking that to my sense of self-worth and personal value. Today, I am in a better place emotionally, physically, financially, and mentally. I accept my experiences as unique to me. Yes, I was part of a family unit through marriage, but I am also an individual in my own right. I hold many roles personally and professionally, but ultimately, it is about accepting and respecting myself unconditionally. I am worthy.

I admit I feared being alone again. I wondered how I would cope after being part of a couple for so long. But funny enough, after all I have been through, I now celebrate being single, and I will expand on that in the next chapter.

The key message I want to share is this: do not make the same mistake I did. Remember your self-worth. If people do not respect you, they are not worth your time or energy, because they add no value to your life. Surround yourself with those who care, where you feel safe and not judged. That is where your true, authentic self can shine.

First, learn to love and respect yourself fully, the good, the bad, and everything in between, because only then can you truly love and respect others.

I know I keep returning to this point, but personal therapy as part of my training has helped me deeply understand myself. I am proud of who I am, and I remind myself daily that my thoughts and feelings are what matter most. Because I am okay, I can be there for others unconditionally.

My Top Tips

- Give yourself time and space for YOU alone. Prioritising "me-time" is not a luxury. It is a vital part of self-care. Even small moments of pause can make a big difference.
- Write down what matters to you. Clarifying what is important and what you want to do helps keep your goals and values in focus. It is your life. Define it on your terms.
- Remember: people's opinions are not facts. What others say or think is a reflection of them, not you. Do not let someone else's comment become your inner critic.

Chapter Eleven: Singlehood and Being Okay with This

In the previous chapter, I mentioned my fear of being single again and wondered how I would cope with it. The more I explored those feelings, the more I realised that what I was really afraid of was the shame associated with being divorced, not the state of being single itself. Looking back now, I can laugh at this, but at the time, it was frustrating. Often, when I met someone and mentioned I was divorced, the response would be, "Don't worry, you're young. You'll find someone else soon." That made me feel like being single was not right, that the norm, or expectation, was to be part of a couple or unit.

For a while, I retreated into a sort of hibernation, keeping to myself. Looking back, I realise I was probably grieving, though I did not understand that at the time. I did not want to explain what was happening or have to justify my feelings to others. I was just beginning to come to terms with the changes in my life and needed space to adjust in my own way.

This time also helped me reorganise my life so that when my son was with me, my focus was fully on him, and I cherished every minute. That time was incredibly meaningful, and I was conscious of wanting to minimise any negative impact on his development. When he was not with me, I used the time and space to sort other parts of my life out.

I also found the courage to reconnect with friends I valued but had lost touch with during my marriage. Thankfully, those friendships have stood the test of time and continue to support me today.

Moving back in with my parents, who already had their own social lives, made me reflect on what I truly wanted going forward. It also meant I could devote more time to my career. Days without the school run allowed me to stay late at work if needed, and I was grateful for that flexibility.

Gradually, I found solace in my own company. On weekends when my son was not with me, I began engaging in activities I had not been able to enjoy before. One day, I came across a local trekking group and decided to give it a try because I loved being outdoors. It always made me smile.

But joining a group alone made me anxious. What if I did not fit in? What if I did not enjoy it? Thankfully, my love for trekking pushed me out of my comfort zone. I gave it a shot with the fallback that if I did not like it, I would not go again. I am so glad I did, because through trekking, I met some wonderful friends who remain close to me today.

I discovered that I actually enjoyed being single again. I noticed more and more people around me who are single by choice. In fact, I read that the Office for National Statistics reported a 16 per cent rise in single-person households between 1997 and 2017, with this number expected to increase further by 2039.* This trend reflects what I have seen personally: more people choosing single life, more divorces, and a reduction in the stigma around both divorce and being single.

So yes, initially I feared being single again and worried about coping. But it is like riding a bike. Even if you have not ridden in a while, you get back into it quickly. On this occasion, I embraced and celebrated my singlehood. I felt gratitude and contentment living a more peaceful and independent life. I considered myself lucky in many ways.

I think the idea that single people must be unhappy or difficult because they have not "found someone" is rubbish. The real key is being content within yourself.

I wanted to be as honest as possible in sharing this chapter because I hope my experience resonates with others and helps normalise these feelings. I am glad I found trekking because it led me to friendships that have become part of my inner circle, friendships I treasure to this day.

*Reference: Office for National Statistics. *Families and households in the UK*. [Online]. Office for National Statistics; 2023. bit.ly/41TjDif

My Top Tips

- Use this time to do what truly matters to you. Choose activities that feel meaningful, not just what is expected, but what brings you a sense of purpose or joy.
- Spend time with yourself. Solitude can be powerful. You might be surprised by what you discover when you slow down and really listen to your own thoughts and feelings.
- Practise self-acceptance, both the positives and the challenges. True change begins when we acknowledge all parts of ourselves without judgement. Acceptance is not the end. It is the starting point for growth.

Chapter Twelve: The 3 L's: Meaning of Love, Life and Laughter

I love the growing trend of acronyms, so naturally, I created one of my own: the 3 L's, Love, Life, and Laughter. These three words carry deep meaning for me and mark a turning point in my personal journey.

Love

It felt fitting to place this chapter here because if it had not been for my love of trekking, I might never have taken that first step out of the four walls I had started isolating myself in. I could have easily stayed in that space, disconnected and stuck, but something inside me knew I needed a change. Looking back now, I realise I was doing something for myself, something I enjoyed. It was a form of self-care, even though I did not label it as such at the time.

I have always loved nature. There is something about fresh air, open space, and being surrounded by greenery that brings peace to my often overactive mind. At that time, I discovered a newly formed community group organising trekking walks. Because it was local and felt safe, I gave it a go, and I am so glad I did. It was exactly what I needed. Trekking allowed me to focus on my breathing, clear my thoughts, and just be. I even made some amazing friends through it, friendships that remain close to me today.

So here is my advice: if there is something you love, be it baking, painting, reading, or anything that brings you joy, make time for it. Losing yourself in something meaningful is, to me, a powerful form of mindfulness. You do not need to be an expert at it. You just need to be present. And do not be afraid to try something new. If trekking sounds unfamiliar or even intimidating, try it. You never know what doors it might open.

But above all, when I reflect on where my greatest strength came from during the most difficult time in my life, my divorce, the answer is clear: my deep, unconditional love for my son.

My therapist once told me she saw my love for him as pure, and that word stayed with me. It resonated deeply because it is pure. I often reflect on our journey, my journey as a mother, and I am sure that my strength was drawn from him. He was always on my mind, my motivation to keep going.

It is hard to describe the connection I feel with my child. It is almost spiritual, like a deep gut instinct. I know him. I sense his moods, his joys, his worries. I never thought of myself as particularly maternal until I became pregnant. That changed everything.

Of course, he is not a baby anymore. He is taller, stronger, and smarter than me. But in my eyes, he will always be my baby. I do not think this deep connection is a result of my divorce. I have always felt it. It is just more pronounced now.

The Oxford Dictionary defines love as a strong feeling of affection and care. But to me, love is something even more powerful. It is unbreakable. It is the feeling I get when I think of his cheeky smile. It warms my heart every time.

Love, though, is not just about romantic relationships. Through my healing, I have come to understand love in many forms, in friendship, in family, in community. True love, in any form, should be unconditional. It accepts, supports, and uplifts. And when someone loves you like that, it brings out the best in you.

Life

It took time, but I slowly began to realise that being a mum, while central to my identity, was not my only identity. I had lost parts of myself along the way and had to rediscover what life meant to me. I had dreams, goals, and a world I still wanted to explore.

I believe we all have a purpose. Some find theirs early in life; others, like me, discover it later. For many of us, it is only through loss or hardship that we start to see what really matters. I wish it did not have to be that way, that we did not need tragedy to see how fortunate we are, but sometimes pain is what wakes us up to life's beauty.

Today, I practise a simple gratitude ritual each night. I will share more on that in the chapter on mindfulness. But this small act has shifted my mindset profoundly.

I now feel I have found my purpose: to support others who have experienced loss and trauma. Through my student placement at Cruse Bereavement Support, I have gained a deeper understanding of grief, a universal experience we will all encounter. It is not easy, but you will get through it. You can find joy again. And doing things that are meaningful to you can be the very thing that keeps you moving forward.

Laughter

The final "L", laughter, may sound light, but it is anything but trivial. I truly believe laughter is medicine for the soul.

I say this now, from a place of healing and strength. But I acknowledge that in the middle of pain, laughter can feel impossible. When I was going through my divorce, the most painful part was the fear of being separated from my son. We had never spent a day apart, and the thought of not seeing him every day broke me.

But I got through it.

I realised that love does not vanish with distance. Our bond could not be broken by time or space. In fact, it became stronger. And sometimes, laughter helped lighten that emotional load. I vividly remember dancing around to Taylor Swift's *Shake It Off*, and even now, that song makes me smile. Sometimes, just shaking out that negative energy is enough to reset your day.

And little by little, I began to laugh again. I found me again.

Final Reflection

I feel incredibly fortunate to have made it through one of the hardest times in my life and come out stronger. Rebuilding myself was not easy. It took time, support, and courage. I often felt alone, and that is what has driven me to share my story, so others know they are not alone.

And before I close this chapter, I want to acknowledge the other love that has helped me along the way, my dearest friend, my soul sister. We have been friends since the age of 11, and only recently have I learned to be more open with her about my emotions. Our friendship is built on honesty, acceptance, and love. That, too, is a powerful form of connection, one that continues to nurture me.

And with that, we naturally move on to the next chapter, relationships.

My Top Tips

- Learn to love yourself unconditionally before trying to love others fully. You are worthy, as you are.
- If you love someone, tell them. Share moments, make memories, and do things that bring mutual joy.
- Write down what you enjoy, and challenge yourself to try something new.
- Live your life fully. You only get one chance. Do not waste it worrying about things that do not matter.
- YOLO, You Only Live Once. Let that be a reason to be bold, brave, and present.

Chapter Thirteen: Meaningful Relationships

As human beings, we are social creatures. We thrive in connection with others, in communities, families, friendships, and partnerships. We are at our most resilient and most fulfilled when we feel seen, supported, and connected.

For me personally, a healthy, meaningful relationship far outweighs wealth, status, or social standing. During difficult times in my life, it was the people I was closest to who held me up, those who allowed me to be fully myself, without judgement. These relationships gave me the courage to sit with my vulnerability and feel safe in my own skin.

Recently, I found myself reflecting on my school years and realised something powerful. I told my soul sister, a friend I have known for over three decades, that it was she who kept me sane during that time. She offered me the kind of emotional comfort I did not know I needed then. Only now, through therapy and deep personal reflection, do I fully understand how much she mattered, and still matters, to me. It is relationships like these that have added colour, depth, and meaning to my life.

The Power of Presence

During my divorce, when I was in a state of emotional shock, it was my younger sister who quietly stood by me. I was not fully present in those moments, but she was, and that presence alone spoke volumes. There was an unspoken trust and a genuine offer of support that I will never forget. It is often in your lowest moments that you come to realise who truly matters in your life.

I also think about my former boss, who remains a close friend to this day. We do not need to speak all the time, but when we do, it is like no time has passed. We simply pick up where we left off. That is the beauty of some relationships. They do not require constant maintenance, only mutual respect and trust.

To me, a meaningful relationship is one built on care, trust, acceptance, and a sense of emotional safety. It is a relationship where you feel seen, valued, and never judged, where you can show up as your whole self, flaws and all.

Support in Unexpected Places

When I reflect on how I coped with my trauma, I realise that it was the support of those close, meaningful relationships that got me through, even before I had any professional therapy. And while I wonder how I might have felt had I accessed therapy at the time, I am incredibly grateful for the therapeutic support I received later on, during my training.

Having personal therapy, particularly as part of becoming a therapist myself, allowed me to understand myself more deeply. It also helped me appreciate the importance of having a real connection with your therapist. When you feel emotionally safe and unjudged, that is when true healing can begin. My therapist challenged me in ways that helped me grow and reflect honestly on my patterns and beliefs.

In today's world, therapy is evolving, with AI and virtual therapy becoming more common. While I can see the benefits of accessibility and convenience, for me, the human connection mattered. Speaking to another human being made the experience more real, more grounded.

Relationships as Part of Well-being

I have said it before, and I will say it again: meaningful relationships are essential to our well-being. They are our emotional anchors, our safety nets when life feels unsteady. Whether it is family, friends, colleagues, or a therapist, having people you trust and feel safe with makes all the difference.

And just as important as having those relationships is nurturing them, showing appreciation, communicating honestly, and recognising the value they bring to your life. After all, everyone likes to feel acknowledged and loved.

My Top Tips

- Think about your relationships. Which ones are truly meaningful to you? Who makes you feel safe, accepted, and supported?
- Reflect on any relationships that feel lost or distant. Are there people you miss, or connections you would like to repair?
- Remember: rupture does not mean the end. Sometimes the strongest relationships are those that have been through difficulty and found a way to heal. It is the repair that builds depth and trust.

Chapter Fourteen: Meaning of Work, Success and Wealth

When I was going through my divorce, I had a busy, demanding job, and in hindsight, I am truly grateful for that. At the time, I did not realise it, but work became one of my most valuable support systems. That is why I believe so strongly in the importance of finding meaning in the work we do.

Having a job that kept me engaged helped me not just mentally, but emotionally, too. It gave me purpose, structure, and a place to focus my energy. Getting out of the house, exercising my mind, and being part of something beyond my personal pain gave me a much-needed break from overthinking. In many ways, work became a quiet anchor that helped keep me steady when everything else felt uncertain.

Why Meaningful Work Matters

I have always had a strong work ethic. That has not changed. I am passionate about what I do, and I find fulfilment in knowing that I can make a difference, whether to an individual, a team, or an organisation. My background is in Human Resources (HR), which, as you can imagine, comes with its fair share of people-related challenges.

During the time of my divorce, I was working in the education sector for an Academy Trust. I was part of a small HR team of four, and we were always busy. I mentioned my former boss earlier, someone who remains a good friend to this day. At that time, she was both understanding and demanding. But there was mutual respect, and that made all the difference.

Having such a demanding job helped keep my mind focused elsewhere. I was not left dwelling on my pain or consumed by "what if" thoughts. I had a purpose during the day, and in the evenings, I was busy caring for my son. By the time I got into bed, I was too tired to spiral into negativity.

I eventually moved on from that job after my line manager left, and was fortunate to stay in the education sector. I took a part-time role at a wonderful, not-for-profit independent school in London, originally intending to stay just one year while managing childcare and navigating the divorce. Eight years later, I am still there, proud to be part of a nurturing and respectful work culture.

This job has been the longest period of employment in my career, which only reinforces my belief that when your work has meaning, it supports not only your finances but also your mental health, emotional well-being, and personal growth.

Redefining Success and Wealth

Reflecting on all this made me think more deeply about happiness and success. What do these words actually mean to me now?

Let us start with definitions:

• Happiness (Oxford): the state of being happy or flourishing; well-being, good fortune, or personal contentment.

• Success (Oxford): the achievement of a desired outcome, goal, or purpose; often associated with wealth, status, or recognition.

In my younger years, I measured happiness and success in very conventional ways: a big house, a stable marriage, children, and a high-profile career. That vision was shaped by my upbringing, culture, and societal expectations. But today, my definition has changed.

Now, success and happiness mean something much simpler and more profound: being content, having good health, nurturing meaningful relationships, and living with purpose and peace.

Sure, success and happiness are technically different. But for me, they are deeply interlinked. I have learned that both begin within. If you are constantly chasing external validation, the job title, the car, the perfect family photo, without feeling at peace with yourself, it never feels like enough.

Now, happiness and success, to me, are about:

- Having a healthy mind and body
- Maintaining honest, loving relationships
- Doing work that feels purposeful
- Creating memories with people I care deeply about

And more than anything, I believe that each of us must define success and happiness for ourselves. No one else can determine that for you.

We are all on a journey to find inner peace, a universal desire to be free from suffering and to feel whole. In today's world, with endless demands and pressures, finding balance within has never been more important. That is where mindfulness helped me, and I will be sharing more on that in the next chapter.

My Top Tips

- Can you find meaning in your current job or role? If not, what changes, big or small, might help you get there?
- What support is available in your workplace? Could you speak with HR or your manager about flexibility or adjustments to support your well-being?
- Reflect on your own definitions of happiness and success. Are they truly yours, or influenced by external expectations?
- Take time to set goals that feel meaningful. What do you want to achieve, and what small steps can help you get there?

Chapter Fifteen: Mindfulness and How This Worked for Me

At the end of my first year of training to be a therapist, our coursework required us to present something meaningful to us. Two areas stood out for me: emotional intelligence and mindfulness. I had recently attended a brief mindfulness training, and I was intrigued by the concept. I wanted to explore it further. Was it just another wellness trend, or could it truly support my development, both as a therapist and as a person?

So, I decided to experiment on myself.

What I discovered was powerful. Mindfulness not only benefited my clients and enhanced my skills as a therapist, but it also supported my personal growth and well-being. That is why I feel compelled to share this experience with you.

What Is Mindfulness?

There is a wealth of material available on mindfulness and its benefits. For those unfamiliar, I find McKenzie's definition particularly helpful:

"Mindfulness is the practice of paying attention, knowing where your attention is, and being able to choose where to direct it."

In essence, mindfulness helps us become more aware, physically, mentally, emotionally, and spiritually. It is about connecting the mind, body, and spirit, and embracing ourselves as whole human beings. It encourages us to respond to our experiences rather than react to our thoughts. That distinction was a game-changer for me.

Being of Indian origin, I had grown up aware of meditation. It was not a new concept to me. In fact, it has deep, ancient roots in Eastern teachings. The unity of mind, body, and spirit has been central to Buddhist philosophy for over 2,600 years. In that tradition, mindful meditation was a tool to reduce suffering through self-discovery, compassion, and spiritual growth.

What made mindfulness particularly accessible in the Western world was its non-religious, low-cost, and scientifically validated approach. Over the last 60 years or so, an increasing body of research has highlighted the effectiveness of mindfulness in improving well-being, emotional regulation, and even brain structure.

My Personal Journey with Mindfulness

After reading an article titled "Mindfulness Meditation Training Changes Brain Structure in 8 Weeks" (ref), I felt even more inspired to try it for myself. I began practising mindfulness meditation in December 2024.

As I researched further, I was excited to learn that there are several mindfulness-based therapeutic approaches. I also discovered the power of breath in regulating both the body and mind. I began incorporating simple breathing techniques and body-awareness practices into my routine.

While I would not say I meditate every single day, I have intentionally integrated mindfulness into my daily life. I can now comfortably sit on the floor for 20 minutes and focus inward. This small but consistent practice has made a noticeable difference in how I feel and how I show up, both personally and professionally.

Mindfulness aligns naturally with my core belief in the interconnectedness of the mind and body, but it has also taught me to be more present in the moment. I am learning to self-regulate, to ground myself, and to observe without judgement. More importantly, I am developing a deeper understanding of myself.

Mindfulness in Everyday Life

What surprised me most was how mindfulness started to appear in small, everyday moments, brushing my teeth, washing the dishes, walking, or even eating. These ordinary tasks became opportunities to practise being fully present.

Another practice that has become part of my evening routine is a simple gratitude exercise. Before I go to sleep, I reflect on the events of the day and internally say, "I am thankful for this." Often, this brings a smile to my face and a warm, happy feeling inside. It has helped me consciously shift my thinking patterns in a more positive direction.

What I Have Learned

Researching and engaging with mindfulness meditation has given me not only a deeper understanding but also a genuine respect for the practice. It has helped me develop greater self-acceptance, be kinder to myself, and stay more grounded, all qualities that support me in my personal and professional life.

Here is what I know to be true:

Mindfulness meditation is a powerful tool. The evidence is clear. It works.

But here is the catch:

It takes time, effort, energy, and discipline.

It is simple, but not always easy.

Mindfulness as a Holistic Tool for Well-being

Ultimately, mindfulness offers a holistic approach to well-being. It does not just benefit our mental health. It nurtures our emotional and spiritual growth, too. It gives us the space to pause, to reflect, and to connect more authentically with ourselves and the world around us.

Final Thoughts

Mindfulness has become more than just a practice for me. It is a way of living. It has helped me be more present, more grounded, and more compassionate, both with myself and with others. Whether you are a therapist, a student, or simply someone navigating life's ups and downs, I believe mindfulness can offer you something meaningful, too. Why not give it a try?

My Top Tips

- Read up on mindfulness meditation, especially if you are new to it. Understanding the principles helps you get started.
- Write down activities you enjoy or feel passionate about. These can also be turned into mindful practices.

- Look for local mindfulness or meditation groups or events. Connecting with like-minded individuals can be inspiring.
- Carve out time for yourself, either in the morning or evening, to reflect on your day and practise gratitude.

Chapter Sixteen: Therapy and How This Worked for Me

I have mentioned before how therapy has been beneficial for me, but the surprising part is that I have only fully realised its value now, nearly seven years after my divorce.

At the time, when I was going through one of the most traumatic experiences of my life, I never even considered therapy. Looking back, I believe this was influenced by both my cultural background and my upbringing. I often wonder: would things have been different if I had therapy then? That is a question I will never know the answer to, and one I have made peace with.

It was not until I began training to become a qualified therapist myself that therapy entered my life in a meaningful way. As part of the course requirements, I had to undergo personal therapy. This was my first experience of it and, hand on heart, it has been transformative. It has given me invaluable insights into myself and has played a key role in supporting my overall well-being.

I want to take a moment to acknowledge my personal therapist, who has been absolutely brilliant. I felt a genuine connection with her, and I cannot stress enough how vital that connection is. It is the foundation of a trusting and meaningful therapeutic relationship. That sense of safety allowed me to open up, explore my feelings, and reveal my vulnerable side.

Through personal therapy and my studies, I have come to better understand my past and my lived experiences. I have been able to make meaning of those experiences, which has supported greater self-awareness and helped me understand myself on a much deeper level.

Therapy, alongside other tools such as Cognitive Coaching and Restorative Practice, has also enhanced my appreciation for the power of language, how we use it, how it shapes our thoughts, and how it influences our relationships. More importantly, it has helped me recognise that I am in control of my own responses. This psychoeducation has shown me how unconscious patterns from my past have shaped my present behaviours.

There is now growing awareness in many workplaces about the connection between the unconscious and conscious mind, and the importance of self-awareness. Modalities such as mentoring, cognitive coaching, and mindfulness are being increasingly used to help people think differently, appreciate diverse perspectives, and become more tolerant and innovative in how they live and work.

For me personally, therapy has supported significant personal growth. I have asked myself: would I have acted differently during my divorce if I had therapy back then? The truth is, I do not know. I might not have even been open to the idea, especially if it came with an added cost. But knowing what I know now, and having experienced the benefits of therapy first-hand, I truly believe it should be offered as a form of support during difficult life transitions, like divorce. Sometimes, just having someone to talk to can make a world of difference.

At this stage in my life, I have come to understand my past, which has allowed me to be more conscious of my actions in the present and to shape the change I want for my future. I know that everyone's experience of divorce, or any life challenge, is unique. I also no longer shy away from the word divorce, and I believe it is important to break the myths and taboos that still surround it in some communities.

We all have a past. What I have learned, and what I hold most dear, is that understanding your past is what allows you to grow. It enables you to live more fully in the present and intentionally shape your future.

If you feel the need to seek professional help, do not be afraid to take that step. The beauty of therapy is that it is open to anyone. As therapists, we are trained to be non-judgemental and to hold space for all experiences. While I have shared my story through the lens of my divorce, therapy can support you through many different challenges and phases in life.

My Top Tips

- Read up on therapy, especially if you are new to it. Understanding the principles can help you feel more prepared and open.
- Find an accredited therapist. Look for professionals listed on official directories such as BACP or other regulatory bodies.
- Do not be afraid to ask for help. Seeking support is not a weakness. It is a step towards healing and self-awareness.

Final Thoughts

We now live in a world where families come in many forms. The traditional idea of a family unit, mum, dad, and two children, is no longer the only norm. I am part of the growing statistic of divorced individuals. I became a single parent and, eventually, part of a blended family, an experience that at first felt daunting, both for my son and me.

What I have come to realise is that therapy can play a crucial role in helping individuals and families navigate these life transitions. As I have shared earlier, it took me nearly seven years to feel ready to talk openly about my experience. A big part of that journey was meeting my partner, who also went through a divorce. While his experience was simpler than mine, there was a shared understanding between us. Together, we focused on creating a secure and stable base for all our children, and I believe we have succeeded in doing just that.

I am grateful every day that I met someone who is kind, understanding, and brings joy into our lives. His support made the hard work we put into building a life together feel far less difficult. And when I think about what family truly means, for me, it is not just about blood. It is about love, trust, and meaningful, supportive relationships.

Looking back, I admit that before my own divorce, I did not really think about what others go through in these situations, the emotional toll, the financial strain, the deep, often hidden, impact on mental health. You could say I was simply ignorant. The process was far more gruelling and drawn out than I ever imagined.

But I got through it.

It took immense courage, strength, determination, and energy to rebuild my life, to reconnect with who I once was and discover who I truly am. Divorce showed me who really mattered and helped me realise what I value most. I found a strength within myself that I never knew existed. And today, I no longer feel shame in being labelled a divorcee. Instead, I feel proud. Proud that I came through one of life's toughest challenges, stronger, mentally, emotionally, and spiritually.

My hope is that by sharing my experience, I can offer some support or insight to others who may be facing their own journey.

We all walk our own unique paths, and the world around us is changing fast. One thing that remains constant is the need to prioritise well-being, mental, emotional, and spiritual. We are each responsible for our own self-care. This is not selfish. It is essential. When we care for ourselves, we build resilience, and this, in turn, helps us manage the inevitable ups and downs that life brings.

I have read the scientific research on mindfulness and meditation, and I have experienced its benefits first-hand. I genuinely believe it can help us reconnect with ourselves and develop a deeper understanding of who we are, as individuals and as human beings.

In today's interconnected world, we are all global citizens. By practising compassion, empathy, and openness to different perspectives, we can not only shape our own futures but also positively influence the generations to come.

About the Author

Bejal Shah is a Humanistic Integrative Therapist and a member of the BACP, with a particular interest in trauma, grief, loss, and overall wellbeing. **She** believes that through compassion, empathy, and an openness to difference, individuals can not only shape their own futures but also positively influence generations to come.

Her work is grounded in valuing and supporting each client in developing greater self-awareness and personal growth. Bejal works collaboratively, offering bespoke and flexible support tailored to individual needs. **She** recognises that life can be challenging and aims to provide a safe, respectful, and supportive space for exploration, understanding, and healing.

To find out more, please visit **mbstherapy.uk**

Printed in Dunstable, United Kingdom

80232159R00048